# *Dear Parent:*
## *Your child's love of reading starts here!*

Every child learns to read in a different way and at his or her own speed. Some go back and forth between reading levels and read favorite books again and again. Others read through each level in order. You can help your young reader improve and become more confident by encouraging his or her own interests and abilities. From books your child reads with you to the first books he or she reads alone, there are I Can Read Books for every stage of reading:

### SHARED READING
Basic language, word repetition, and whimsical illustrations, ideal for sharing with your emergent reader

### BEGINNING READING
Short sentences, familiar words, and simple concepts for children eager to read on their own

### READING WITH HELP
Engaging stories, longer sentences, and language play for developing readers

### READING ALONE
Complex plots, challenging vocabulary, and high-interest topics for the independent reader

### ADVANCED READING
Short paragraphs, chapters, and exciting themes for the perfect bridge to chapter books

**I Can Read Books** have introduced children to the joy of reading since 1957. Featuring award-winning authors and illustrators and a fabulous cast of beloved characters, I Can Read Books set the standard for beginning readers.

A lifetime of discovery begins with the magical words **"I Can Read!"**

# The BEST TEACHER in Second Grade

story by Katharine Kenah
pictures by Abby Carter

SCHOLASTIC INC.

New York  Toronto  London  Auckland  Sydney
Mexico City  New Delhi  Hong Kong  Buenos Aires

*To Virginia Simons,*
*the real BEST TEACHER in Room 75, with love*
*—K.K.*

*To Samantha and Carter*
*—A.C.*

ISBN-13: 978-0-545-03638-2
ISBN-10: 0-545-03638-0

Text copyright © 2006 by Katharine Kenah.
Illustrations copyright © 2006 by Abby Carter. All rights reserved.
Published by Scholastic Inc., 557 Broadway, New York, NY 10012, by arrangement with HarperCollins Children's Books, a division of HarperCollins Publishers Inc. I Can Read Book® is a trademark of HarperCollins Publishers Inc. SCHOLASTIC and associated logos are trademarks and/or registered trademarks of Scholastic Inc.

22 21 20                                                      19 20 21 22 23 24/0

Printed in the U.S.A.                                                      40

First Scholastic printing, September 2007

# Contents

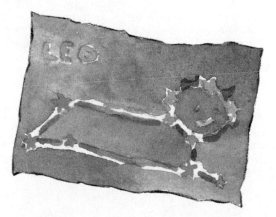

# Luna's Idea

Luna had the best teacher
in second grade.
Mr. Hopper loved the sky
*almost* as much as she did.

Luna had been scared
to move to a new school
in the middle of the year.
But after one week,
she had a poem about planets,
a painting of twinkling stars,
and pencils the color of the sun.
Room 75 was a blast!

On Friday Mr. Hopper said,
"Family Night is in two weeks.
We need to plan a special show.
Does anyone have an idea?"

"A talent show," said Nina.

"A cooking show," said Ollie.

"A hamster show!" shouted Sam.

George Washington, their pet,

was running in his wheel.

Luna thought about
what she loved most.
She looked up at the sky.
She looked down
at her painting of stars.

She looked at the telescope
in the corner of Room 75.
Then Luna smiled
and raised her hand.

13

"We could do a show
about the night sky," said Luna.
"Planets follow a path,
like tightrope walkers.
Comets shoot through space.
And there are animal shapes
in the star constellations.
It is like a midnight circus."
Mr. Hopper grinned.
"I know what you mean," he said.

Everyone else stared at Luna
like she was the new kid
from outer space.

Suddenly Ollie shouted, "A circus!
What a great idea!"
"I've always wanted to swing
on a trapeze," said Sophie.
"I'll be the ringmaster," said Miguel.
"My grandpa has a top hat."

"Those are all fine ideas,"
said Mr. Hopper.
"A circus it is!"
"But I said a *midnight* circus,"
called Luna. "Not a regular circus."
No one was listening.
Her good idea had come and gone,
just like a shooting star.

# Lions and Tigers and Bears

On Monday Mr. Hopper said,

"We have a lot to do this week.

Please work in your groups.

Lions make circus masks.

Tigers make circus tickets.

Bears make circus posters.

Have fun!"

The Bears got out paint
and paper, glitter and glue.

"I'm going to paint three ladies on fancy horses," said Sophie.

"I'm going to paint two monkeys on motorcycles," said Miguel.

"I'm going to paint George Washington jumping through a hoop," said Sam.

Luna unrolled a sheet
of midnight blue paper.
"I am going to paint a lion,"
she said.
Luna painted ten gold stars
and sprinkled them with glitter.

"That is not a lion," said Ollie.

"Yes, it is," Luna said. "Watch!"

She connected the stars with paint

and formed the shape of a lion.

"Meet Leo, the lion constellation,"

she said.

Everyone stared at Luna.

At recess on Wednesday,
Luna twirled three hoops
around her waist.
"Guess what I'm going to be
in our circus," she called.

"An animal trainer?" asked Sam.

"A clown?" asked Sophie.

"The planet Saturn, with its rings!" cried Luna.

Everyone stared at Luna.

On Friday they pushed their desks

into a circus ring.

"What does the ringmaster do?"

asked Sophie.

"He runs the show," said Miguel.

"And shines in a spotlight,"

said Luna.

"Just like the Man in the Moon."

"Good answers," said Mr. Hopper.

But Luna saw people laughing at her.

She felt as small

as a speck of dust in space.

That night Luna peeled

the glow-in-the-dark stars

from her bedroom walls.

She peeled off the sun

and the moon and the comets

and threw them in the trash.

Then Luna shoved her telescope
deep into her closet
and hated the sky until Monday.

# The Lunch Line

At lunchtime on Monday,

the Lions and Tigers and Bears

slid their trays along the counter.

Mrs. Mudlark's class

was at the front of the line.

They were talking about animals

and clowns.

As Luna reached for a milk carton,
someone bumped into her.
"Sorry," said the girl.
"I was practicing my spin."

"Why?" asked Luna.

She said, "Because I am going to be a dancing lady on a horse in our Family Night circus."

Mrs. Mudlark's class was putting on
a *circus* for Family Night!
The Lions and Tigers and Bears
raced back to Room 75
with the news.

"Now there will be two circuses
on Family Night," said Nina.
"I knew we should have planned
a cooking show!" groaned Ollie.
"What can we do?" cried Sophie.
Mr. Hopper said, "I think someone
in this room has the answer."

"Mrs. Mudlark's class is putting on
a *regular* circus," said Luna.
She took a deep breath and smiled.
"I have an idea."

Everyone stared at Luna.

Everyone was listening.

# The Midnight Circus

At seven o'clock on Family Night,

Room 75 was crowded and noisy.

Parents and grandparents

sat on small chairs.

Brothers and sisters

peeked in desks

around the circus ring.

Outside in the hallway,

the Lions and Tigers and Bears

held bright hoops

and wands of sparkling stars.

They pushed Miguel toward the door

and said, "Go on. Go on!"

Miguel marched into Room 75
with a top hat on his head.

"LATE AT NIGHT," he announced,
"WHEN YOU ARE FAST ASLEEP,
THE MIDNIGHT CIRCUS BEGINS.
THE MAN IN THE MOON
LEADS THE WAY
AS THE STAR PERFORMERS
MOVE IN."

"Will they know we are
the night sky?" asked Nina.

"Sure," said Luna.

"How?" asked Nina.

Luna whispered, "Because we are
all second-grade stars."

"Here we go," said Mr. Hopper.

He walked into Room 75

with a huge cardboard moon.

Step by step, star by star,

the others followed him in.

The Family Night audience
clapped and cheered.
Babies woke up and laughed.

For one whole hour,
Luna's class turned Room 75
into a midnight circus.

When it was over, Mr. Hopper said,

"Good work! I am proud of you all."

Then he looked at Luna and smiled.

"Thank you for your fine idea."

Luna beamed like the sun.

She had the best teacher

in second grade.